ENKI BILAL

GODS IN CHAOS

TITAN BOOKS

LONDON

«Immortality is a form of dictatorship of life over death--since I am a dictator and alive, all that remains is for me to become immortal. And this I will become! If it kills me!»
J.F. Choublanc
«Miscellaneous Writings»
Paris, 2023

Other books by Enki Bilal (Coming soon):
The Woman Trap
The Town Which Did Not Exist
Phalanxes of the Black Order
The Hunting Party

Other Titan Books in this series:
The Airtight Garage by Moebius
Arzach and Other Fantasy Stories by Moebius
The Gardens of Aedena by Moebius
Joe's Bar by Carlos Sampayo and José Muñoz
The Last Voyage of Sindbad by Jan Strnad and Richard Corben
The Long Tomorrow and Other Science Fiction Stories
by Moebius
The Magician's Wife by Jerome Charyn and Francois Boucq
Upon A Star by Moebius

GODS IN CHAOS
ISBN: 1 85286 050 2

Written and illustrated by Enki Bilal

Published by
Titan Books Ltd,
58 St Giles High St,
London WC2H 8LH.

First Titan Edition, April 1988
10 9 8 7 6 5 4 3 2 1

British edition by arrangement with Catalan
Communications, 43 East 19th Street, New York,
N.Y. 10003, USA.

Copyright © 1980 Dargaud Editeur, Paris by Bilal.
Translation by Tom Leighton.
Edited by Bernd Metz.
Design by Catalan Communications

Printed and bound in Spain by JTV
Dep. L.B. –22.358/87

PARIS- EARLY MARCH 2023.— ON THE EVE OF A NEW BUT MEANINGLESS ELECTORAL MASQUERADE... NOTHING SEEMS LIKELY TO CHANGE IN THE POLITICALLY AUTONOMOUS AND HOPELESSLY FASCIST GREATER PARIS. THE CITY IS DIVIDED INTO TWO TOTALLY UNEQUAL SECTORS... THE FIRST, THE CENTRAL CITY, IS INHABITED BY A SOCIAL ELITE, A MASSIVE REGULAR ARMY AND THE RULING CLASS. THE SECOND SECTOR, SURROUNDING THE FIRST AND EXTENDING OUT BEYOND SIGHT, IS THE CROSSROAD FOR ALL KINDS OF ADVENTURERS AND EXTRATERRESTRIALS SINCE THE TIME A LARGE ASTROPORT WAS PUT INTO SERVICE. THE GOVERNMENT MILITIA PATROLS, AND ONLY SECONDARILY INSURES THE SECURITY OF THIS WORLD OF DEGENERACY, POVERTY AND FILTH. ADDING TO THE USUAL FAKE HUBBUB OVER THE UPCOMING ELECTIONS IS A STRANGE UNEASE DUE TO THE APPEARANCE OF A HUGE, ODDLY PYRAMID-SHAPED SPACESHIP HOVERING OVER THE ASTROPORT. PUBLIC UNREST IS ON THE UPSWING. RUMOR HAS IT THAT THE OCCUPANTS OF THE FLYING PYRAMID ARE DEMANDING ASTRONOMICAL QUANTITIES OF FUEL FROM THE CITY OF PARIS. THE CAUTIOUS (AND SUSPICIOUS) SILENCE OF JEAN-FERDINAND CHOUBLANC, THE PRESENT GOVERNOR, IS NOT REASSURING.

PROBLEMS, GENERAL?

NO, NOTHING ALARMING, GOVERNOR... JUST SOME ROUTINE BUSINESS FOR THE AIR MILITIA...

A BIT MORE KHOL AROUND THE EYES, WILL YOU...

LIKE THIS?

HMM... PERFECT, PERFECT... YOU CAN LET THE GIRLS GO...

WELL, I AM WAITING FOR YOUR CONCLUSIONS, MY FRIEND!

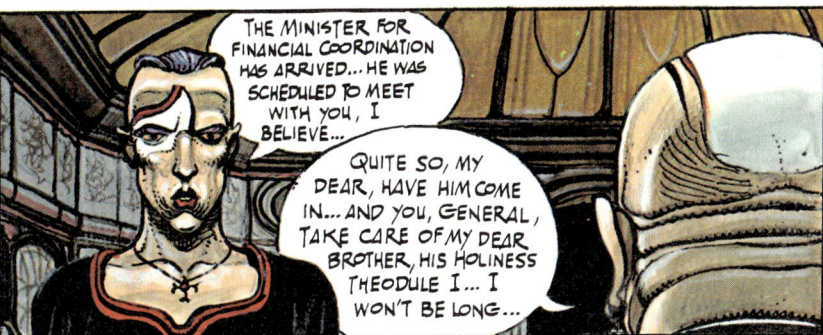

THE MINISTER FOR FINANCIAL COORDINATION HAS ARRIVED... HE WAS SCHEDULED TO MEET WITH YOU, I BELIEVE...

QUITE SO, MY DEAR, HAVE HIM COME IN... AND YOU, GENERAL, TAKE CARE OF MY DEAR BROTHER, HIS HOLINESS THEODULE I... I WON'T BE LONG...

I AM NOT GOING TO HIDE FROM YOU, GOVERNOR, THE FACT THAT THIS BUSINESS LOOKS RATHER UNFAVORABLE... THE FUEL NEEDS OF THESE... UH... OF THESE BEINGS ARE MUCH TOO VAST AND THE LACK OF ANY FINANCIAL EXCHANGE OR OTHER ASSET, MAKES THIS DEAL BIZARRE AND DANGEROUS AT BEST...

LISTEN TO ME, THE NATURE OF THIS DEAL AND THE EXCHANGE I INTEND TO GET OUT OF IT ARE MY BUSINESS! AS FOR THE FINANCIAL LOSS YOU SEEM TO BE AFRAID OF, THERE ARE DOZENS OF WAYS OF MAKING IT UP... NEW TAXES ON THE ZONES ADJACENT TO THE SECOND SECTOR, DECLARING WAR ON THE WEALTHY BUT MILITARILY VULNERABLE CITIES IN THE EAST, AND THAT'S ONLY FOR STARTERS...

NO, WHAT I WANT TO KNOW FOR NOW IS WHETHER SUCH A TAPPING OF OUR PRESENT FUEL SUPPLIES IS POSSIBLE OR NOT!!

5

... ACCORDING TO MY CALCULATIONS AND MY CABINET'S ESTIMATES, IT IS POSSIBLE... ALTHOUGH WE MUST THEN PLAN ON WAR IN THE NEAR FUTURE TO REPLENISH OUR TREASURY AND OUR FUEL RESERVES...

SHH, SHH...QUIET, GOGOL, QUIET!

PERFECT, MY DEAR FRIEND, THIS IS WHAT I NEED IN ORDER TO NEGOTIATE SOLIDLY WITH THIS JACKAL ANUBIS AND HIS BARNYARD COURT ...YOU MAY GO NOW.

GOGOL!

GOD WILL RECOGNIZE HIS OWN IN THE TEST OF STRENGTH IN WHICH YOU MUST PARTICIPATE, JEAN-FERDINAND CHOUBLANC, GOVERNOR OF THE AUTONOMOUS CITY OF PARIS, AGAINST THIS UNCONTROLLABLE, IRREVERENTLY PAGAN COALITION OF SATAN WORSHIPERS WHO DARE, IN THEIR INFERNAL OUTLANDISHNESS, TO PROCLAIM THEM- SELVES DIVINE AND ETERNAL...

FOR THE PROTECTION OF OUR HOLY CITY, FOR THE PRESERVATION OF HER RACIAL PURITY AND IN THE INTEREST OF EACH AND EVERYONE OF US, MAY YOU SUCCEED IN YOUR NOBLE MISSION IN THE NAME OF GOD, ONE AND IMMUTABLE...

NHEW..

ARE THESE... UH... THESE CHERUBS COMING WITH US, GOVERNOR?

I'M AFRAID SO, GENERAL...

MY POOR BROTHER, THEODULE I, IS COMPLETELY OUT OF HIS MIND... HE HAS DECIDED THAT THESE LITTLE WINGED BEASTS FROM OUR COLONY OF DIPHDA HAVE BEEN SENT TO HIM BY GOD HIMSELF... THAT THEY'RE ANGELS OF SOME KIND...

...ANGELS IN CHARGE OF KEEPING AN EYE ON ME AND EXORCISING THESE PRETENDED EGYPTIAN DIVINITIES...OBVIOUSLY HE HAS NOT DIGESTED THIS HARSH BLOW TO HIS CONCEPT OF A UNIQUE AND UNIVERSAL GOD...

I SEE...

ELYSEE POSTE A

MEANWHILE 9,000 TO 12,000 FEET ABOVE...
OBJECT SIGHTED AT 13:00...
YOU'RE TALKING ABOUT A KIND OF A WHAT... A PREHISTORIC SPACE CAPSULE...
YEAH... AND STILL NOT A SOUND OUT OF IT...
WATCH OUT, I'M GOING TO FIRE!
GO AHEAD!

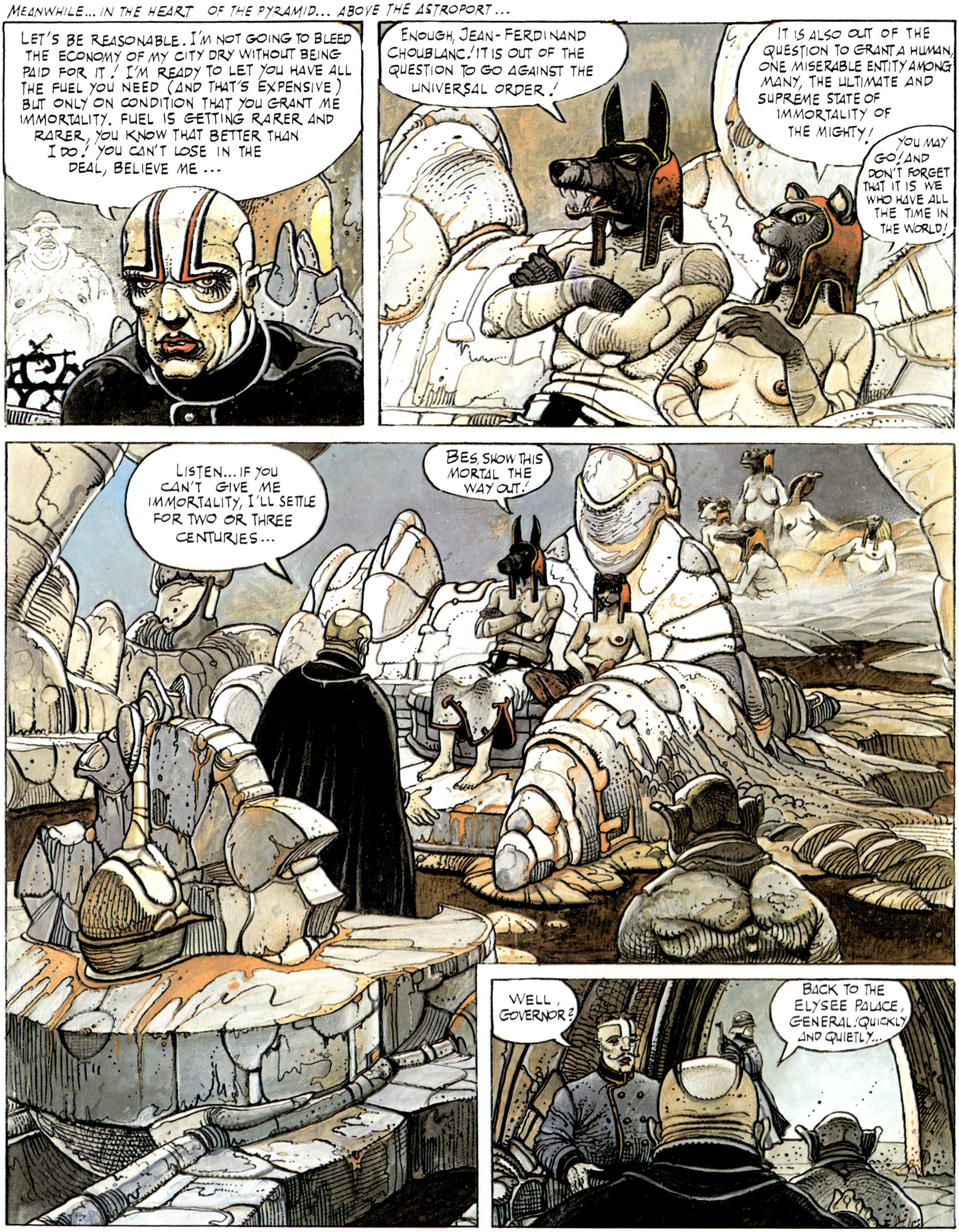

LET'S BE REASONABLE. I'M NOT GOING TO BLEED THE ECONOMY OF MY CITY DRY WITHOUT BEING PAID FOR IT! I'M READY TO LET YOU HAVE ALL THE FUEL YOU NEED (AND THAT'S EXPENSIVE) BUT ONLY ON CONDITION THAT YOU GRANT ME IMMORTALITY. FUEL IS GETTING RARER AND RARER, YOU KNOW THAT BETTER THAN I DO! YOU CAN'T LOSE IN THE DEAL, BELIEVE ME...

ENOUGH, JEAN-FERDINAND CHOUBLANC! IT IS OUT OF THE QUESTION TO GO AGAINST THE UNIVERSAL ORDER!

IT IS ALSO OUT OF THE QUESTION TO GRANT A HUMAN, ONE MISERABLE ENTITY AMONG MANY, THE ULTIMATE AND SUPREME STATE OF IMMORTALITY OF THE MIGHTY!

YOU MAY GO! AND DON'T FORGET THAT IT IS WE WHO HAVE ALL THE TIME IN THE WORLD!

LISTEN... IF YOU CAN'T GIVE ME IMMORTALITY, I'LL SETTLE FOR TWO OR THREE CENTURIES...

BES, SHOW THIS MORTAL THE WAY OUT!

WELL, GOVERNOR?

BACK TO THE ELYSEE PALACE, GENERAL! QUICKLY AND QUIETLY...

"THE LAWFUL VOICE"
OFFICIAL PRESS
CIRCULATION 75,000

"ORDER"
OFFICIAL PRESS
CIRCULATION 60,000

AN ENEMY SHIP SHOT DOWN

Yesterday, March 2, late afternoon, a foreign and apparently hostile ship was masterfully destroyed by two Stridents of the Air Militia, flown by pilot Commanders Jules Bourdonnier and Arthur Deslors. The occupant of the machine managed to parachute out at the last minute, but was welcomed by the Ground Militia Forces, and quickly put out of commission.

It should be noted that this hateful character, most likely a spy from the cities of the East, lost a leg in the fall. The militia, in a spirit of generosity, left this leg out for food for the miserable creatures of the Second Sector South who had swarmed like so many hungry flies around the scene of the action.

Militia General Vertegoutte, on his return from the pyramid, where he had accompanied Governor Jean-Ferdinand Choublanc, expressed his deep satisfaction with "this remarkable joint action taken by the Air and Ground Militia Forces".

PYRAMID: NEGOTIATIONS BEGUN AGAIN

After receiving a special papal blessing in the Holy Chapel of the Elysee Palace, the Governor of the City of Paris, Jean-Ferdinand Choublanc, accompanied by Militia General Vertegoutte, went to the flying pyramid which has been parked for nearly two weeks now over the Paris-South Astroport. This resumption of negotiations (the 3rd) is once again due to the efforts of our beloved Governor whose will to safeguard the interests of our city and whose diplomatic finesse grow more forceful as problems continue... Problems which in this instance are shown to be especially thorny. After three hours of heated discussions with the mysterious occupants of the pyramid whose nature and identity have been kept secret for obvious reasons of national security, Jean-Ferdinand Choublanc returned to the Governmental Elysee Palace where he made the statement: 'I have no statement to make. Just have confidence in me!''. That we have, Governor.

EFFICIENCY OF AIR MILITIA

A mysterious flying object which violated our air space was brilliantly intercepted by two Air Militia fighters yesterday, March 2, late in the afternoon. The Air Militia is constantly on the alert for our security.

"ORDER"

"PEOPLE'S RESISTANCE"
FRINGE PRESS
MAKESHIFT
CIRCULATION
40 TO 50

DA MYSTERIOUS FALLING

Da mysterious falling has happen in our town on evening March 2 da man parachuted freezed solid he was so much so he leg broke clean when he hit. they filthy Choublanc militia (late like usual) got fucked cause da freezed mystery man flapped off before arrival of them.

ha ha ha

SORTIE

CALM DOWN!

AAAAAH!

MY LEG!!! GOD, WHERE'S MY LEG!??

WHO'D YOU SAY?

HORUS! THE ONE TO WHOM YOU OWE THE PROLONGATION OF YOUR MISERABLE MORTAL LIFE... THE ONE WHO IS GOING TO DO YOU THE HONOR OF LIVING IN YOUR BODY, THE ONE WHO KNOWS ALL, ALL ABOUT YOUR POOR LIFE OF A DESERTER, ALCIDE NIKOPOL!

I SAID, CALM DOWN, YOU PITIFUL HUMAN, AND LISTEN TO WHAT I, HORUS, GOD AMONG THE GODS, IMMORTAL AMONG THE IMMORTALS, HAVE TO SAY TO YOU...

16

NIKOPOL... ALCIDE NIKOPOL!? HEY, THAT'S MY NAME.!!? WHO ARE YOU FOR GOD'S SAKE, AND HOW DID I GET HERE?!!

...HERE, IN PARIS! I RECOGNIZE IT.! THE METRO, ALESIA STATION, IN THE FOURTEENTH! IN FRANCE.! ON EARTH.!!! GOD, HOW DID I GET BACK TO EARTH ??!

ALESIA

...FOR THE TIME BEING I DON'T KNOW... BUT I DO KNOW THAT IN 1993 A FRENCH MILITARY COURT SENTENCED YOU FOR DESERTION TO BE SHIPPED OUT INTO THE COSMOS WITHOUT HOPE OF RETURNING... WITH THE FIRST TWENTY YEARS OF THE TRIP IN A STATE OF HIBERNATION...

YES, I REMEMBER ALL THAT... AND TODAY, WHAT YEAR IS IT?

2023...

...2023!.. SHIIIT...

WHICH MEANS THAT YOU LEFT YOUR PLANET THIRTY YEARS AGO, SAD MORTAL... AND SINCE I HAVE JUST UNFROZEN YOU, I DEDUCE THAT YOU UNDERWENT AN ADDITIONAL TEN YEARS OF HIBERNATION... MOST SURELY AN ACT OF THIS XB2 WHO WENT ALONG WITH YOU...

XB2...XB2...YES, I REMEMBER... MY GUARD, HE WAS PUNISHED TOO... BUT FOR INSUBORDINATION ...CHIEF-SERGEANT ROBOT XB2...

...AND TODAY, I WAKE UP THIRTY YEARS LATER, AT ALESIA STATION, ONE LEG MISSING, PISSING BLOOD ALL OVER THE PLACE, NEXT TO A NAKED GUY WITH THE HEAD OF SOME BIRD OF PREY WHO KNOWS MY WHOLE LIFE AND PRETENDS HE'S GOD...

GOD, I DON'T UNDERSTAND ANY OF IT ANYMORE! I REMEMBER AS IF IT WAS A YEAR AGO!... 1992... I REFUSED TO FIGHT AGAINST THE SINO-SOVIET COALITION... I DESERTED... I WAS CAUGHT, PUT ON TRIAL, AND A YEAR LATER, SHOT OUT INTO SPACE, IN A FLYING FRIDGE ALONG WITH A PARANOID ROBOT SERGEANT...

I CAN IMAGINE YOUR CONFUSION AND TAKE INTO ACCOUNT YOUR INTELLECTUAL LIMITS UNDER THESE CIRCUMSTANCES, POOR NIKOPOL... I THINK YOU CAN THANK ME, HORUS, GOD OF HIERAKO-NOPOLIS, SON OF ISIS AND OSIRIS, MIGHTY AND UNIVERSAL CREATOR, FOR TAKING CHARGE OF YOU...

I MUST SAY HOWEVER...

OOP.!

HEY, WHERE ARE YOU GOING?

UNDER-STAND NOTHING...

...THAT IN THE COURSE OF THE SMALL EXCURSION TAKEN IN YOUR BODY BETWEEN THE PLACE WHERE YOU FELL AND HERE, I WAS ABLE TO MAKE A RAPID PHYSICAL AND PSYCHOLOGICAL EXAMINATION OF YOUR PERSON... APART THE USUAL DEFECTS OF THE HUMAN RACE, THE RESULTS SEEMED TO ME QUITE SATISFACTORY...

SATISFACTORY.!!! ARE YOU SHITTING ME.!!? MAIMED, ONE-LEGGED FOR LIFE, AND YOU FIND THAT SATISFACTORY!!?

COMPLETELY SATISFACTORY... YOUR BODY IS IN PERFECT CONDITION COMPARED TO THE BODIES OF THE WRETCHES I HAVE HAD TO INHABIT THESE PAST FEW DAYS... SICKNESS AND MUTATIONS ARE EATING AWAY THE QUARTERS ADJACENT TO THIS CITY... HEALTHY BODIES ARE RARE... THE ONE I LEFT FOR YOURS BELONGED TO A FANATIC WHO BELIEVED IN ONE GOD... HIS BRAIN BECAME UNCONTROLLABLE... YOUR ARRIVAL WAS PROVIDENTIAL, BELIEVE ME...

AAH, IT HURTS...

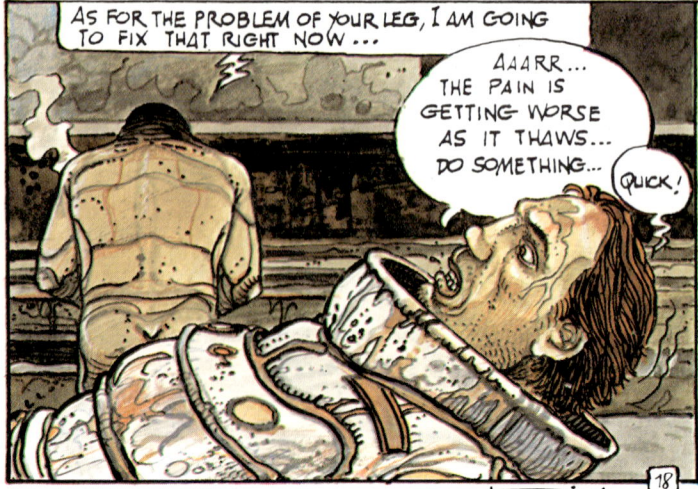

AS FOR THE PROBLEM OF YOUR LEG, I AM GOING TO FIX THAT RIGHT NOW...

AAARR... THE PAIN IS GETTING WORSE AS IT THAWS... DO SOMETHING...

QUICK!

BILAL 18

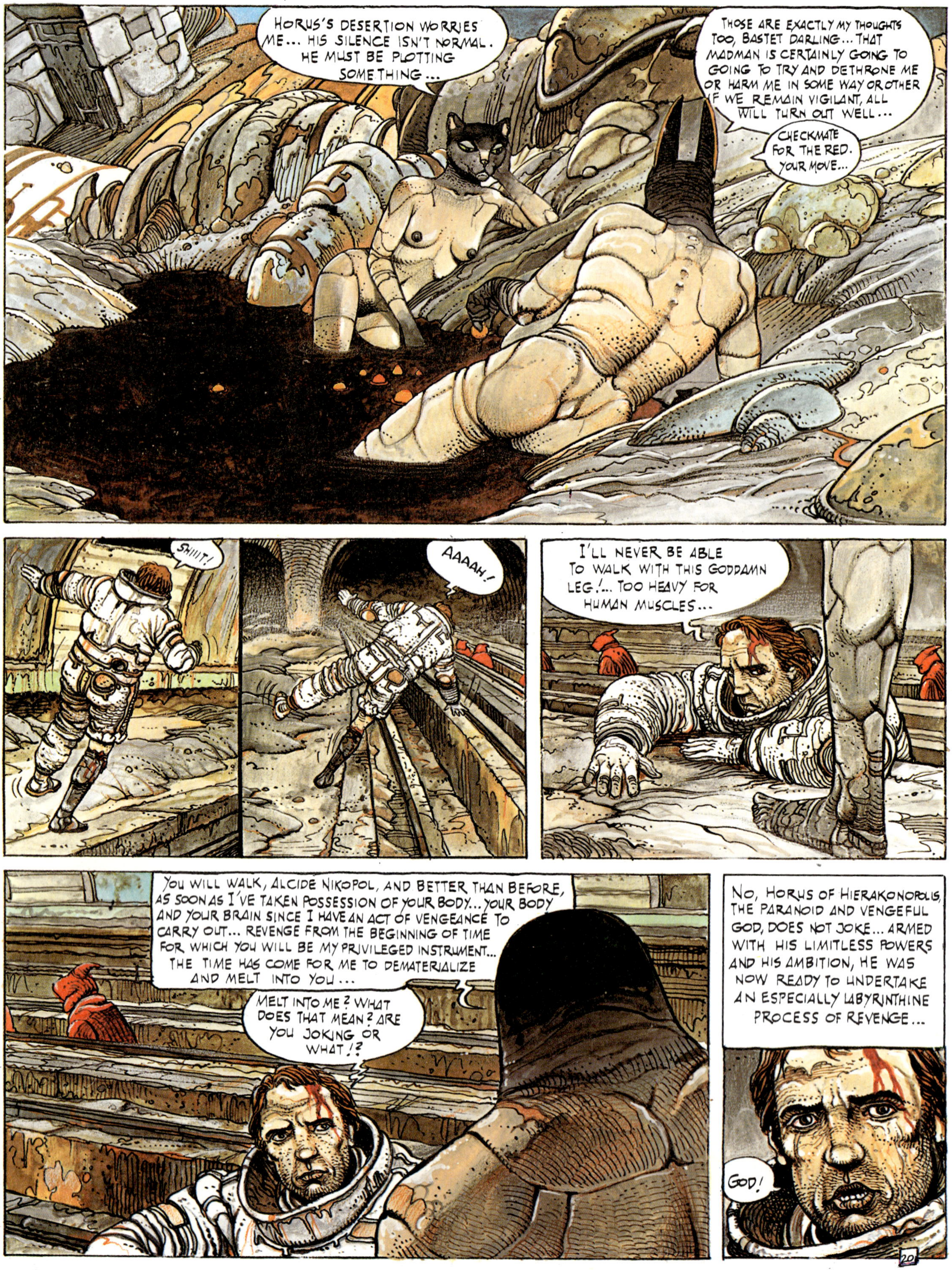

HORUS'S DESERTION WORRIES ME... HIS SILENCE ISN'T NORMAL. HE MUST BE PLOTTING SOMETHING...

THOSE ARE EXACTLY MY THOUGHTS TOO, BASTET DARLING... THAT MADMAN IS CERTAINLY GOING TO GOING TO TRY AND DETHRONE ME OR HARM ME IN SOME WAY OR OTHER IF WE REMAIN VIGILANT, ALL WILL TURN OUT WELL...

CHECKMATE FOR THE RED. YOUR MOVE...

SHIIT!

AAAAH!

I'LL NEVER BE ABLE TO WALK WITH THIS GODDAMN LEG!... TOO HEAVY FOR HUMAN MUSCLES...

YOU WILL WALK, ALCIDE NIKOPOL, AND BETTER THAN BEFORE, AS SOON AS I'VE TAKEN POSSESSION OF YOUR BODY... YOUR BODY AND YOUR BRAIN SINCE I HAVE AN ACT OF VENGEANCE TO CARRY OUT... REVENGE FROM THE BEGINNING OF TIME FOR WHICH YOU WILL BE MY PRIVILEGED INSTRUMENT... THE TIME HAS COME FOR ME TO DEMATERIALIZE AND MELT INTO YOU...

MELT INTO ME? WHAT DOES THAT MEAN? ARE YOU JOKING OR WHAT!?

NO, HORUS OF HIERAKONOPOLIS, THE PARANOID AND VENGEFUL GOD, DOES NOT JOKE... ARMED WITH HIS LIMITLESS POWERS AND HIS AMBITION, HE WAS NOW READY TO UNDERTAKE AN ESPECIALLY LABYRINTHINE PROCESS OF REVENGE...

GOD!

THUS ON MARCH 3, 2023, AT METRO STATION ALESIA, TOOK PLACE THE POSSESSION OF THE BODY OF ALCIDE NIKOPOL BY HORUS OF HIERAKONOPOLIS.

HORUS OF HIERAKONOPOLIS, GOD, DEMATERIALIZED.

ALCIDE NIKOPOL, HUMAN, COMPLETELY OVERCOME.

PASSERSBY.

GET UP, NIKOPOL... YOU CAN WALK NOW... I AM IN YOU!

I... I... DON'T BELIEVE IT... YOU'RE BLUFFING...

YOU ARE A FOOL, NIKOPOL

FOOL YOURSELF!

EVERYTHING IS READY, GENERAL. THE GOVERNOR'S ARMCHAIR WILL EXPLODE THIS EVENING AT EXACTLY 9 P.M., JUST BEFORE HALF-TIME...

VERY GOOD, MY FRIEND... YOU HAVE OF COURSE TAKEN INTO ACCOUNT MY PRESENCE BESIDE THE GOVERNOR AT THE MOMENT OF THE EXPLOSION!?

REST ASSURED, GENERAL, IT WILL NOT REALLY BE AN EXPLOSION... I HAVE BEEN ABLE TO OBTAIN FROM ONE OF THE ALPHERATZIEN HANDLERS AT THE ASTROPORT OF VARECH OF FOMALH-AUT... A SIMPLE ELECTRIC SPARK SUFFICIENT TO TURN THIS SUBSTANCE INTO A DEADLY HIGH-ENERGY ONE... THE GOVERNOR WILL BE SEATED THIS EVENING ON A KIND OF ELECTRIC CHAIR... YOU WILL BE IN NO DANGER, GENERAL...

GOOD.

MY OFFICERS AND THEIR MEN WILL BE READY AS WELL... AND FROM THIS EVENING ON, POWER WILL HAVE CHANGED HANDS... MY FRIEND, THIS CALLS FOR A CELEBRATION! A DROP OF OLD COGNAC?

HE IS TRULY PRECIOUS TO ME, BUT, GOD, IS HE UGLY...

NO THANK YOU, GENERAL, I NEVER TOUCH ALCOHOL.

A.M.T.

WE MUST QUICKLY FIND YOU SOME NEW CLOTHES... YOU WILL BE SPOTTED AND PICKED UP WITH THIS SUIT ON...

GOOD LORD, HAS PARIS EVER CHANGED...

NORMAL, AFTER 30 YEARS AND TWO NUCLEAR WARS...

STILL... WHAT A SHOCK...

22

YOUR FUNNY TELEPATHIC BEAST DOES NOT LIKE ME AT ALL ... BUT, STRANGELY ENOUGH, HE IS THE ONE WHO IS SAVING MY LIFE ...

SHHH, SHHH, QUIET, GOGOL, QUIET!

YES... HE HAS A NIMBLE BRAIN AND A SHARP EAR... THANKS TO HIM THE PLOT THIS EVENING WILL BE FOILED. THE SECURITY DEPARTMENT IS WORKING ON IT AS WE SPEAK ... I WILL THEN TAKE CHARGE OF PURGING AND RESTRUCTURING THE MILITIA...

QUIET, GOGOL!

...STILL I DIDN'T EXPECT ANYTHING LIKE THAT FROM VERTEGOUTTE...

HAH, THE DOG!

AAAAH!

GOGOL !!!

SUPERMARC

LET'S JOIN THIS FARCE OF A FUNERAL PROCESSION... WE'LL FIND SOMETHING TO PUT ON YOU FROM ONE OF THESE SAD MORTALS...

IT GETS BETTER AND BETTER AROUND HERE... THE SUPERMARKET WHERE I USED TO SHOP HAS BEEN TURNED INTO A CEMETARY...

THIS GUY AHEAD OF US SHOULD DO THE TRICK... HE'S JUST ABOUT YOUR SIZE ...

I'M WARNING YOU I HATE USING VIOLENCE...

A BASIL CHOUBLANQUISME FASCISTIQUE

YOU'LL USE WHAT I TELL YOU WHEN I TELL YOU TO... DON'T FORGET THAT I HAVE THE POWER TO DISCONNECT YOUR BRAIN CELLS, NIKOPOL!

YOU'RE THE LOWEST!

I KNOW...

BILAL

No doubt about it, you're hopelessly childish, my poor friend...

Huh... Just put yourself in my place...

Hey, dere Mistah Nikopol's back...

!?!
?

Clementine!!! God, my little Clementine, here, in this grave, dead!

He gone crazy...

CLEMENTINE MORGANIDON 1968 - 2021

You're losing your grip, Nikopol... Come on, let's get going...

Good ding got ole Gorgon. He dere watchin over da grave you mudder... gone two months, dats long, ma boy...

What's this all mean? I...

Calm down, don't get upset... do you know this Clementine Morganidon?

Clementine...

This business is very clear... remember, Nikopol... you were supposed to marry this Clementine when the military court sentenced you to be shot into space...

I remember now... we were in love my little Clementine and me...

But what you didn't know was that she must have been pregnant when you left... so this little old man mistook you for your own son...

I have a son and Clementine is dead..

Yes, dead at 53 and she's left you a son with the your name and he's just about the same age you are now...

REINCARNAT GREFFES

MESSES

POUDRE F.
ULVES

CAFE

OEUFS DURS DE MENK
GROS DEMI-GRO

MENKAR 012B

ERIE

DEHORS ILS ENIFFIENS

ERDRE

P.R

25

NIGHT FELL VERY FAST AS IT ALWAYS DID IN MARCH FOR SOME YEARS NOW... A SAD, PAINFUL NIGHT WITH A STRANGE, HEAVY DUMPING OF GREENISH SNOW... ALCIDE NIKOPOL'S CONFUSION WAS EVEN GREATER THAN EVER...

THIS IS THE BORDER POST... BEYOND IS THE FIRST SECTOR ... THE SECTOR OF PRIVILEGE AND LAW...

I DON'T GIVE A SHIT...

NOT ME, NIKOPOL, I DO...

WE'LL QUICKLY GET RID OF THE GUARD, THEN WE'LL CAUSE THE REGISTRATION COMPUTER AND THE DISINTEGRATION MACHINE TO IMPLODE...

IS THAT ALL...

...LIKE THIS? PERFECT!

PSHiiiii

AAAH!!!

I.D.! MAGNETIC PASS CARD...

CERTAINLY!

LOOK HIM STRAIGHT IN THE EYES, NIKOPOL!

CONTROL

YES, TO THE EXTREME... THOSE CHOUBLANQUIST SLOGANS PERFECTLY DEFINE THE SITUATION IN YOUR POOR CITY...

HMMM... THIS CHOUBLANC GUY DIDN'T DIG TOO DEEP... HE'S STOLEN MUSSOLINI'S SLOGANS WORD FOR WORD...

MUSSOLINI?

THE STATE IS EVERYTHING. NOTHING HUMAN OR SPIRITUAL EXISTS OUTSIDE THE STATE.

WAR IS FOR MEN WHAT CHILDBEARING IS FOR WOMEN.

YES... A DICTATOR FROM THE LAST CENTURY... I CAN STILL REMEMBER MY COLLEGE EXAM ESSAY QUESTION FROM 1980..."THE RISE OF FASCISM IN ITALY"... A COMPLETE MESS...

YOU SEE, NIKOPOL, I THINK FINALLY WE ARE GOING TO COME UP WITH A COMMON GOAL... YOURS, POLITICAL AND HUMANITARIAN, AND MINE, PERSONAL REVENGE OF A DIVINE AND UNIVERSAL SCOPE... AT THE BEGINNING I THOUGHT I WOULD HAVE TO DISCONNECT YOUR BRAIN FUNCTIONS IN ORDER TO BE ABLE TO USE YOUR BODY WITHOUT ANY INTERFERENCE, BUT NOW I'M BEGINNING TO SEE THAT A KIND OF... COOPERATIVE EFFORT MAY BE POSSIBLE...

PERSONALLY I CAN'T SEE HOW... AND ANYWAY WHAT IS THIS COMMON GOAL?

FLECHES NOIRES DE PARIS CONTRE BOULETS ROUGES DE BRATISLAVA

SEIZING POWER OVER PARIS IN THE NEXT ELECTIONS... AND EVEN BEFORE THAT IF WE CAN... MAYBE EVEN TONIGHT...

YOU'VE GOT TO BE JOKING?

NO... IN FACT THE FIRST ACT WILL BEGIN RIGHT HERE AND NOW...

28

... A RACE WHICH TODAY EMANATES SUCH PHYSICAL POWER THAT ITS RIGHT TO SPREAD OVER THE WORLD IS AS UNDENIABLE AS THAT OF MIGHTY RIVERS TO FLOW TO THE SEA !!!

LET OUR BLACK ARROWS HEAR WHAT I SAY SO THAT THEY UNDERSTAND THAT ABOVE AND BEYOND TONIGHT'S GAME, WE EXPECT NOTHING LESS THAN FOR THEM TO SYMBOLICALLY CRUSH AN IDEOLOGY THAT IS TOTALLY OUTDATED AND INCOMPREHENSIBLE TO OUR NEW MINDS.

8:15 P.M.

... AND NOW LET THE GAME BEGIN !

THIS BARGAIN-BASEMENT DICTATOR HAS BORROWED IT ALL... WORD FOR WORD FROM IL DUCE...

WHO ?

THE SAME ONE I MENTIONED BEFORE ...

WATCH OUT, I THINK THEY'RE COMING...

THEY WHO?

THE BLACK ARROWS...

GOD, IS THAT IT !? HOCKEY PLAYERS ! WE'RE GOING TO BE WATCHING A HOCKEY GAME !

WE'RE EVEN GOING TO PLAY, NIKOPOL ...

8:38 P.M.

ONLY 22 MINUTES TO GO, HA HA...

PARIS BLACK ARROWS 2, BRATISLAVA RED BULLETS 0

8:45 P.M.

IN A QUARTER OF AN HOUR.

BLACK ARROWS 3, RED BULLETS 0 AND ONE SERIOUS INJURY.

8:56 P.M.

IN FOUR MINUTES...

BLACK ARROWS 3, ONE INJURED (CRITICALLY), RED BULLETS 1, ONE DEAD AND TWO INJURED (ONE SERIOUSLY).

AAAGH!!!

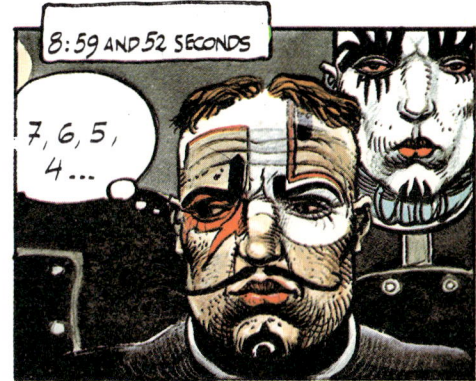

A STUPID GAME, BUT STILL RATHER GRIPPING, ODDLY ENOUGH...

THIS 23 INTRIGUES ME... THERE'S SOMETHING NOT HUMAN IN HIS BEHAVIOR...

YES, HIS STRENGTH IS IN FACT QUITE UNCOMMON AND INCOMPATIBLE WITH THAT OF THE INFERIOR RACES DOWN HERE...

I WONDER WHETHER THE CRIMINAL HORUS HASN'T EXCEEDED HIS RIGHTS AND TAKEN POSSESSION OF THE BODY OF A HUMAN... A DEEP PRESENTIMENT OF THIS IS SHAKING ME TO THE CORE...

34

COME NOW, KHEPRI, UNLESS HIS REASON HAS TOTALLY DISFUNCTIONED, HE CAN NOT HAVE VIOLATED THE ETHICS OF THE MIGHTY TO THIS EXTENT.

KLING

IN ANY CASE THIS WOULD BE AN EVENT WITHOUT PRECEDENT IN THE UNFATHOMABLE HISTORY OF ETERNITY...

...FROM NOW ON EVERYTHING IS POSSIBLE WITH HIM; EVEN DEMATERIALIZATION INTO A INFERIOR, MORTAL BEING... HORUS IS CRAZY, NOBLE FRIENDS...

KLING

THAT'S ALSO MY OPINION, BUT DON'T YOU HEAR SOMETHING THAT KEEPS BANGING AGAINST THE HULL OF OUR VESSEL...?

A METALLIC SOUND, I'D SAY...

9:38 P.M.... TIME CALLED, GAME OVER... THE SCORE 7 TO 4 IN FAVOR OF THE CZECHOSOVIETS...

NOW FOR THE SECOND PHASE...

9:39 P.M. JEAN-FERDINAND CHOUBLANC, ANGRY AND BITTER, SUDDENLY LEAVES THE OFFICIAL BOX...

9:40 P.M. END OF THE TELEVISION BROADCAST...

LET'S BE CAREFUL, FRIENDS OF UNIVERSAL HEAVEN, THE MALICIOUSNESS OF HORUS OF HIERAKONOPOLIS IS EQUAL ONLY TO HIS MADNESS...

KLING KLING

INTERLUDE

THAT ANNOYING NOISE JUST DOESN'T STOP...

BES! GO FIND OUT WHAT THAT NOISE IS!...

NIGHT CAME DOWN HEAVY AND IMPENETRABLE... SWEPT HERE AND THERE BY SULFUREOUS WINDS...

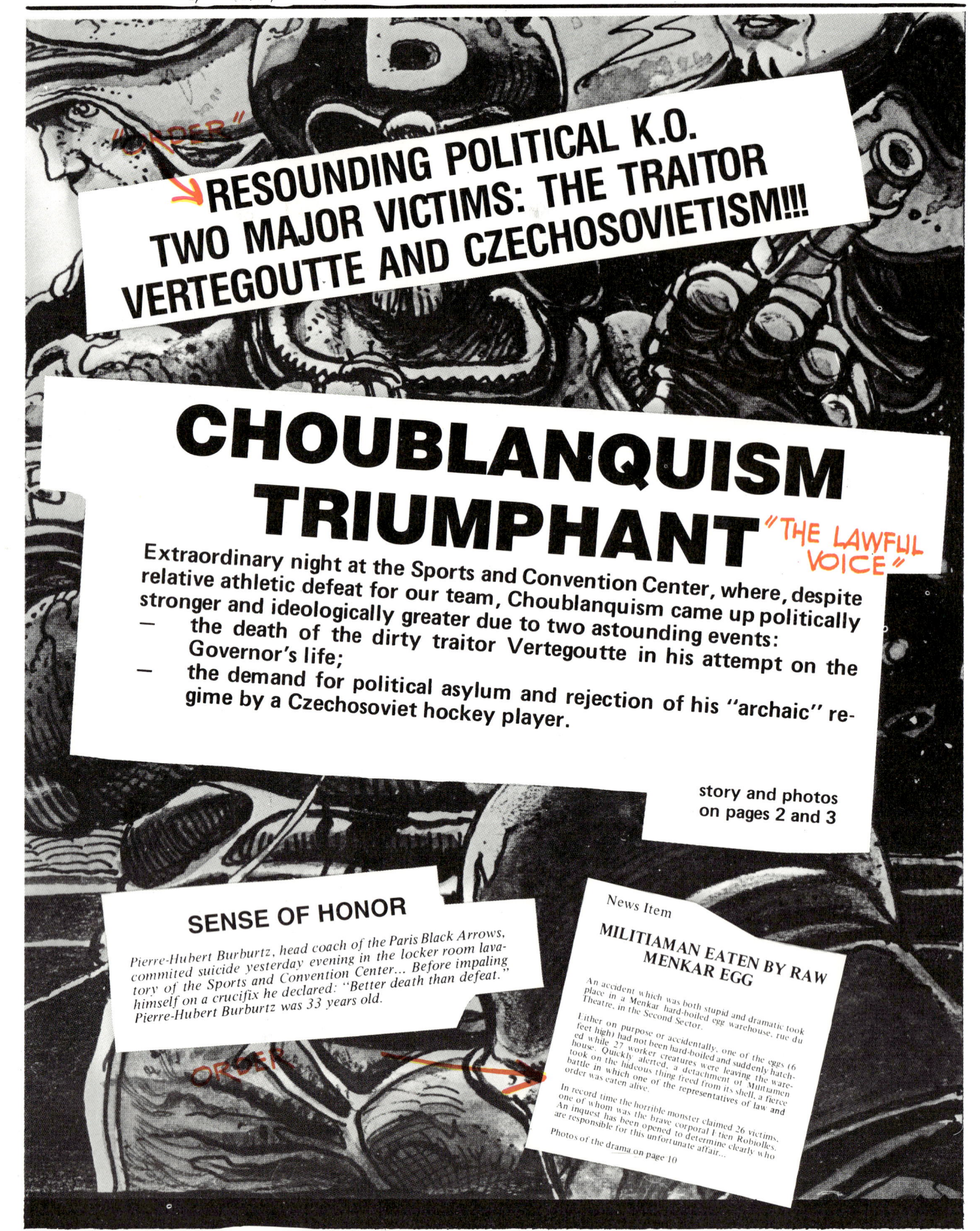

"ORDER"

RESOUNDING POLITICAL K.O.
TWO MAJOR VICTIMS: THE TRAITOR VERTEGOUTTE AND CZECHOSOVIETISM!!!

CHOUBLANQUISM TRIUMPHANT

"THE LAWFUL VOICE"

Extraordinary night at the Sports and Convention Center, where, despite relative athletic defeat for our team, Choublanquism came up politically stronger and ideologically greater due to two astounding events:

— the death of the dirty traitor Vertegoutte in his attempt on the Governor's life;

— the demand for political asylum and rejection of his "archaic" regime by a Czechosoviet hockey player.

story and photos
on pages 2 and 3

SENSE OF HONOR

Pierre-Hubert Burburtz, head coach of the Paris Black Arrows, commited suicide yesterday evening in the locker room lavatory of the Sports and Convention Center... Before impaling himself on a crucifix he declared: "Better death than defeat." Pierre-Hubert Burburtz was 33 years old.

ORDER

News Item

MILITIAMAN EATEN BY RAW MENKAR EGG

An accident which was both stupid and dramatic took place in a Menkar hard-boiled egg warehouse, rue du Théâtre, in the Second Sector.

Either on purpose or accidentally, one of the eggs (6 feet high) had not been hard-boiled and suddenly hatched while 27 worker creatures were leaving the warehouse. Quickly alerted, a detachment of Militiamen took on the hideous thing freed from its shell, a fierce battle in which one of the representatives of law and order was eaten alive.

In record time the horrible monster claimed 26 victims, one of whom was the brave corporal I tien Robiolles. An inquest has been opened to determine clearly who are responsible for this unfortunate affair...

Photos of the drama on page 10

AUTHOR'S NOTE: "PEOPLE'S RESISTANCE" WILL UNFORTUNATELY NO LONGER BE PUBLISHED... ITS SOLE EDITOR-PRINTER-DISTRIBUTOR WAS ONE OF THE UNFORTUNATE VICTIMS OF THE CRAZY MENKAR EGG...

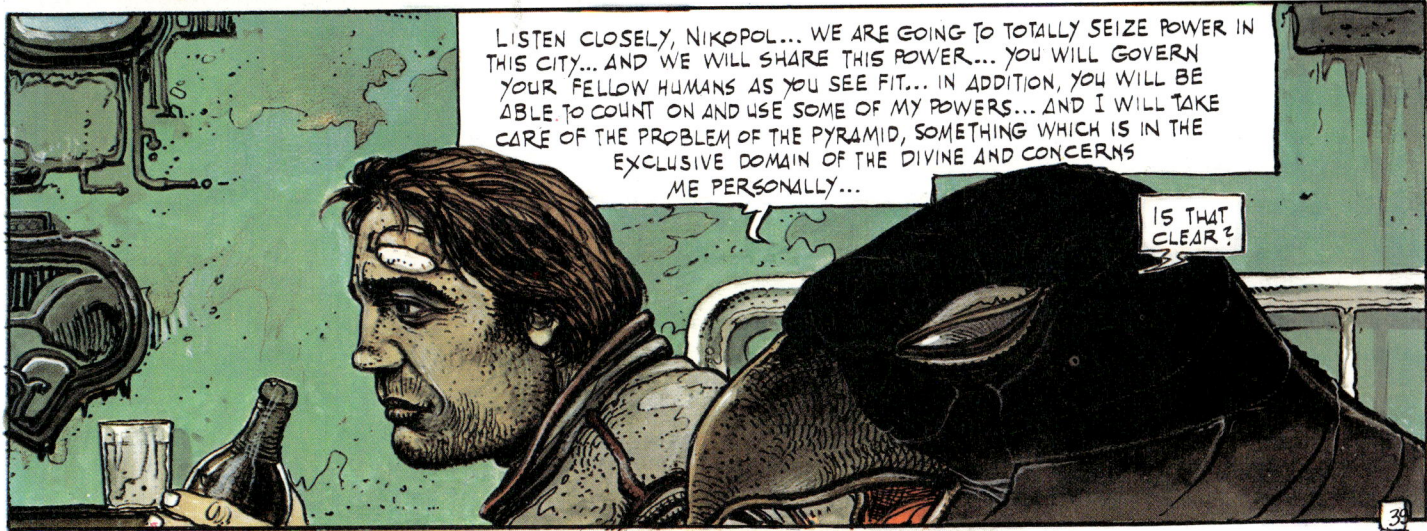

... NOT REALLY... MAYBE I'M NOSEY, BUT JUST WHAT IS THIS PYRAMID PROBLEM ALL ABOUT ANYWAY?..

WHAT YOU ARE ASKING OF ME, NIKOPOL, TOUCHES ON UNIVERSAL VALUES WHICH EARTHLY WORDS WOULD NOT BE ABLE TO EXPRESS...

IN ANY CASE, I CAN TELL YOU THAT DEEP DIFFERENCES, A SAVAGE HATRED OF THOSE OF MY KIND AND UNBRIDLED AMBITION, ON WHICH I FLATTER MYSELF, LEAD ME TO BREAK WITH MY ROOTS... FROM NOW ON I AM WORKING FOR MYSELF, AGAINST THE UNIVERSAL ORDER AND HOLY ETERNITY...

SEIZING POWER IN PARIS IS ABOVE ALL HAVING CONTROL OVER FUEL... WITH SUCH A WEAPON I HAVE WHAT I NEED TO BRING ANUBIS AND HIS CLIQUE OF SLUGGISH HOMEBODIES TO THEIR KNEES...

... PRETTY GROTESQUE FOR GODS TO BE DEPENDENT ON AN OIL PIPELINE ISN'T IT?...

THE TECHNOLOGY OF OUR VESSEL (OF THEIRS I SHOULD SAY) IS VERY ARCHAIC... I ALWAYS WAS IN FAVOR OF ATOMNIONIC EFFICIENCY AS FAR AS PROPULSION IS CONCERNED... LET THEM BITE THEIR NAILS FOR NOW...

BUT I'M AFRAID THAT AN AGREEMENT BETWEEN THE GOVERNOR AND ANUBIS WILL OCCUR BEFORE WE ARE MASTERS OF THE CITY...

TOC TOC

SHIT.!!! SOMEONE'S KNOCKING.!...

QUIET... I AM GOING BACK INTO YOUR BODY...

40

VLOUFFF

HIDE YOUR LEG !!!

TOC TOC TOC

UH, COME IN !!!

...YOU WERE TALKING TO YOURSELF?

UH... NO... I WAS RECITING A POEM BY BAUDELAIRE... I LIKE THAT STUFF A LOT...DON'T YOU?

"REMEMBER, MY SOUL, THE OBJECT WE SAW, THIS BEAUTIFUL SUMMER MORNING SO MILD JUST OFF THE PATH A CARCASS LAY RAW ON A BED STREWN WITH ... "

THAT'S ENOUGH.!!! CLEAN UP, SHAVE AND PUT ON THESE CLOTHES ! THE GOVERNOR WANTS TO INTRODUCE YOU TO THE PRESS...

WELL DONE, NIKOPOL !

MEANWHILE... 2ND SECTOR, ALESIA QUARTER, CEMETARY SUPERMARKET...

SAY THERE, YOU AGAIN, MISTAH NIKOPOL !?!

ICI REPOSE SEBASTIEN BUSE

?

WHAT DO YOU MEAN, ME AGAIN ?

LINGERI

YA BEN HERE YEZADAY, MISTAH NIKOPOL? YA DON'T MEMBAH ? ...

NO ! NO, I DON'T REMEMBER BEING HERE YESTERDAY, GORGON, MY POOR OLD FRIEND...

4

MEANWHILE, BACK INSIDE THE PYRAMID...

... AND WHY BACK ON EARTH AGAINST THE ORDERS OF YOUR SUPERIORS, XB2?

RADIO CONTACT HAD BEEN CUT FOR OVER 18 YEARS... THE "NIKOPOL-HIBER-NATION" EXPERIMENT HAD FALLEN THROUGH AGES AGO...

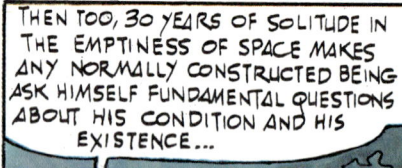

THEN TOO, 30 YEARS OF SOLITUDE IN THE EMPTINESS OF SPACE MAKES ANY NORMALLY CONSTRUCTED BEING ASK HIMSELF FUNDAMENTAL QUESTIONS ABOUT HIS CONDITION AND HIS EXISTENCE...

THAT'S HOW I DISCOVERED THE UNIQUE AND INTOXICATING FEELING OF PERSONAL AMBITION... THIS RETURN TO EARTH IS A NEW START FOR ME AND A NEAR DEFINITIVE BREAK WITH MY FORMER MILITARY VALUES OF THE DUTY-COUNTRY KIND...

WHAT ABOUT THIS NIKOPOL?

... A HARMLESS BEING WITHOUT MUCH SCOPE... HE SHOULD BE DEAD BY NOW...

THAT WILL BE ALL FOR NOW... BES, TAKE CARE OF XB2, WILL YOU?

I DON'T LIKE THIS ROBOT AT ALL, BUT HE COULD BE USEFUL IN HELPING US GET THE FUEL THIS WRETCHED CHOUBLANC DENIES US AND WHICH HE'LL CONTINUE DENYING US IF HE'S RE-ELECTED...

HOW'S THAT, BASTET DARLING?

BY HAVING XB2 ELECTED GOVERNOR!

RIDICULOUS!!! LOOK WHAT I LOOK LIKE IN THIS THING!?

SO, ONCE YOU'RE IN POWER YOU CAN MAKE AND BREAK FASHION ACCORDING TO YOUR WHIM AND TASTES...

FASTER! THE GOVERNOR DOES NOT LIKE TO BE KEPT WAITING!

"LEGS IN THE AIR, LIKE A WOMAN OF LUSTS, BURNING AND SWEATING OUT POISONS, HER BELLY FULL OF BREATHY GUSTS YAWNED WIDE WITH CYNICAL NOTIONS...

... YET YOU WILL BE LIKE THIS EXCRESCENCE, LIKE THIS FILTHY INFECTION, STAR OF MY EYES, SUN OF MY ESSENCE, YOU, MY ANGEL, MY PASSION..."

NOW BEGINS THE SERIOUS PART, NIKOPOL...

I'VE GOT A HEADACHE...

A STROKE OF FATE, THIS DISSIDENT... I MUST GET THE MOST OUT OF THIS AFFAIR, CREATE AN EVENT AROUND THIS ACT OF HIS AND THE POLITICS WHICH GO WITH IT... ...WE COULDN'T HAVE DREAMED OF A BETTER THEME FOR MY CAMPAIGN...

EVERYTHING HAS BEEN PLANNED WITH THIS IN MIND... ALSO, YOUR BROTHER, HIS HOLINESS THEODULE I, WILL BE SUPPORTING YOU... IN A SPECTACULAR WAY, HE'S TOLD ME... THE WAY THINGS ARE GOING NO ONE WILL DARE ENTER THE RACE AGAINST YOU...

HMMM... THAT WOULD MAKE THINGS A LOT SIMPLER... I'VE GOT OTHER IRONS IN THE FIRE, YOU KNOW...

QUIET, GOGOL, QUIET...

THAT ANUBIS AND HIS ADVISERS ARE THE ONES WHO'LL BE DISAPPOINTED WHEN I'M RE-ELECTED... I HAVE A HUNCH THAT THEIR SITUATION IS NOT QUITE AS COMFORTABLE AS THEY WOULD HAVE ME BELIEVE...THEY'LL BE THE FIRST TO GIVE IN...

...AND WILL MAKE ME IMMORTAL (IF GOD WILLS)

I HOPE SO FOR YOU...

44

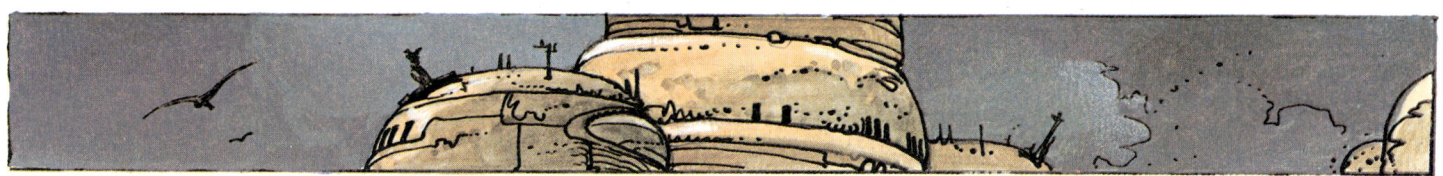

THE DISSIDENT NIKOPOL HAS ARRIVED, MR. GOVERNOR...

HAVE HIM COME IN!

ELYSEE POSTE 1

DEAR FRIEND, I AM HAPPY AND PROUD TO COUNT YOU AMONG MY SUBJECTS... I DEEPLY APPRECIATE YOUR COURAGEOUS AND EXEMPLARY GESTURE, BELIEVE ME... YOU ARE WELCOME HERE...

UH... WE ARE VERY... I MEAN, I AM VERY MOVED BY YOUR HOSPITALITY... ISN'T FREEDOM WORTH SACRIFICING A LITTLE BLOOD AND PAIN?

STOP IT, NIKOPOL!

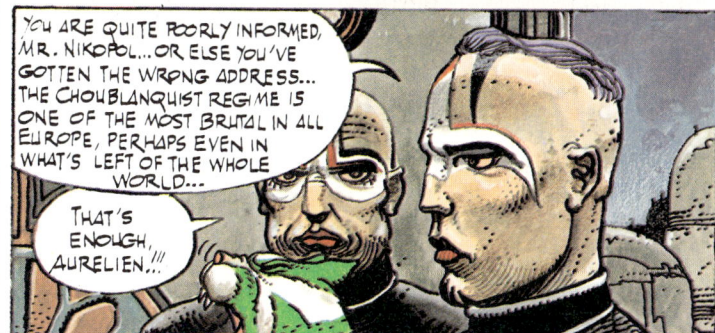

YOU ARE QUITE POORLY INFORMED, MR. NIKOPOL... OR ELSE YOU'VE GOTTEN THE WRONG ADDRESS... THE CHOUBLANQUIST REGIME IS ONE OF THE MOST BRUTAL IN ALL EUROPE, PERHAPS EVEN IN WHAT'S LEFT OF THE WHOLE WORLD...

THAT'S ENOUGH, AURELIEN...!!!

I HAVE A TELEVISED DECLARATION TO MAKE, DEAR FRIEND, AND I THINK IT AN OPPORTUNE TIME TO INTRODUCE YOU TO OUR CITY... WHETHER YOU LIKE IT OR NOT YOU ARE ALREADY PERCEIVED AS A HERO BY MY SUBJECTS... AND DICTATORSHIP, WHICH, YOU MUST KNOW, IS A VERY DIFFICULT ART, NEEDS AN ARTIST OF YOUR CALIBER...

YOU HONOR ME TOO MUCH...

THINGS ARE GOING RATHER WELL, NIKOPOL... I THINK WE'LL BE ABLE TO SKIP A FEW STEPS...

I SEE YOU AS WORKING WITH YOUNG PEOPLE OR IN PROPAGANDA OR SPORTS, AND WITH FERVOR... A DYNAMIC AND GENEROUS POSITION FOR YOU... MADE IN YOUR OWN IMAGE...

I AM TAKING CONTROL OF YOUR BRAIN FUNCTIONS FOR GREATER SECURITY...

...

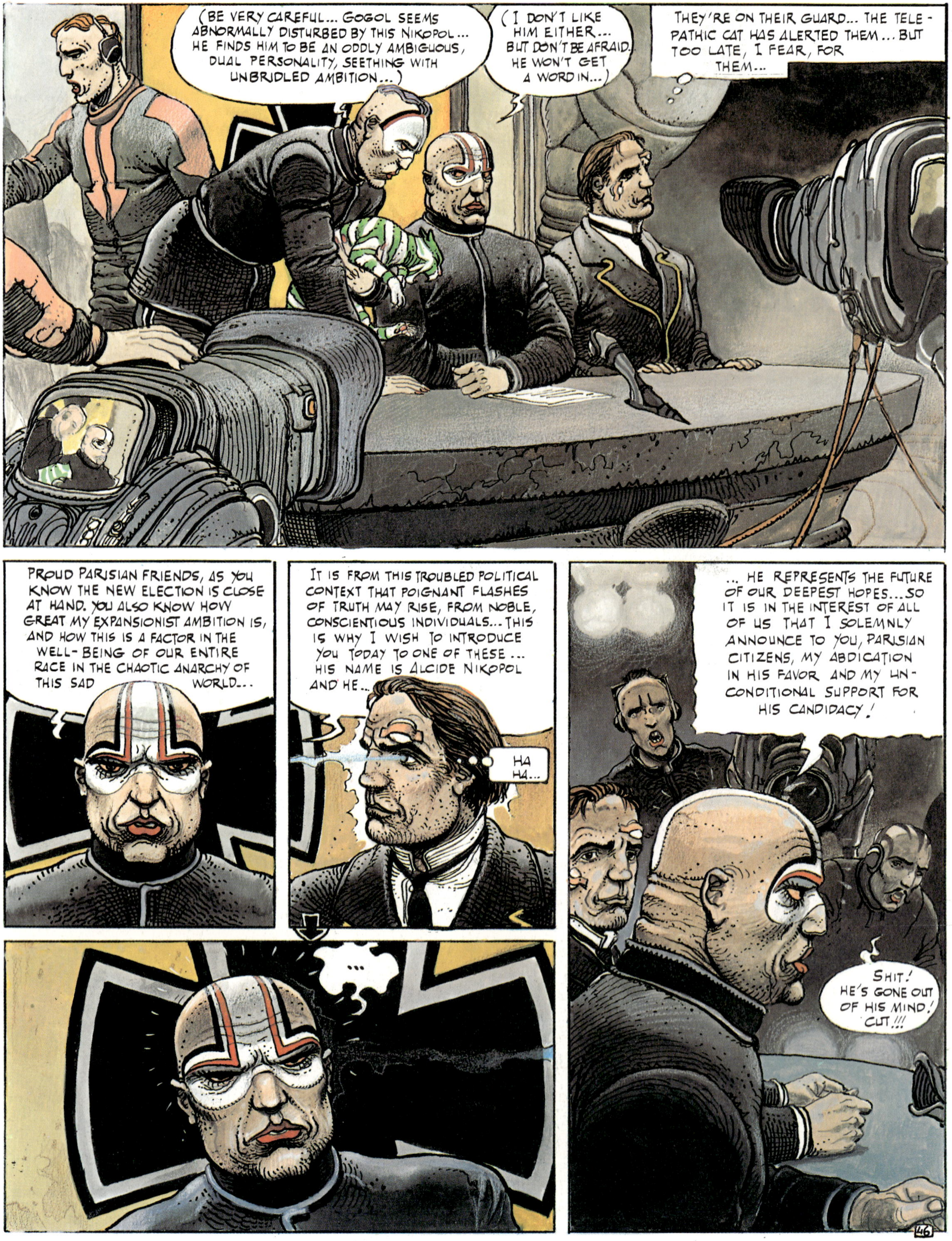

(BE VERY CAREFUL... GOGOL SEEMS ABNORMALLY DISTURBED BY THIS NIKOPOL... HE FINDS HIM TO BE AN ODDLY AMBIGUOUS, DUAL PERSONALITY, SEETHING WITH UNBRIDLED AMBITION...)

(I DON'T LIKE HIM EITHER... BUT DON'T BE AFRAID, HE WON'T GET A WORD IN...)

THEY'RE ON THEIR GUARD... THE TELE-PATHIC CAT HAS ALERTED THEM... BUT TOO LATE, I FEAR, FOR THEM...

PROUD PARISIAN FRIENDS, AS YOU KNOW THE NEW ELECTION IS CLOSE AT HAND. YOU ALSO KNOW HOW GREAT MY EXPANSIONIST AMBITION IS, AND HOW THIS IS A FACTOR IN THE WELL-BEING OF OUR ENTIRE RACE IN THE CHAOTIC ANARCHY OF THIS SAD WORLD...

IT IS FROM THIS TROUBLED POLITICAL CONTEXT THAT POIGNANT FLASHES OF TRUTH MAY RISE, FROM NOBLE, CONSCIENTIOUS INDIVIDUALS... THIS IS WHY I WISH TO INTRODUCE YOU TODAY TO ONE OF THESE... HIS NAME IS ALCIDE NIKOPOL AND HE...

HA HA...

... HE REPRESENTS THE FUTURE OF OUR DEEPEST HOPES... SO IT IS IN THE INTEREST OF ALL OF US THAT I SOLEMNLY ANNOUNCE TO YOU, PARISIAN CITIZENS, MY ABDICATION IN HIS FAVOR AND MY UN-CONDITIONAL SUPPORT FOR HIS CANDIDACY!

SHIT! HE'S GONE OUT OF HIS MIND! CUT!!!

...

HAVE HIM COME IN

"THE LAWFUL VOICE"

SHOCK!
J.F. CHOUBLANC ABDICATES!!!

Political event without precedent. The sitting governor, the much respected Jean-Ferdinand Choublanc, abdicated in favor of a foreigner of doubtful origin and highly suspect behavior.

During the course of a brief televised speech, designed to inaugurate the opening of the electoral campaign, Jean-Ferdinand Choublanc announced his resignation in favor of an undesirable, disturbing individual. 24 hours before the solemn presentation of the candidates (by his Holiness Pope Theodule I in the Church of Notre Dame of Paris) and 8 days before the governmental election this irrational act throws certain mayhem into

AURELIEN BURNOLDZ-MORTIER SPEAKS OUT FORCEFULLY!

Ex-governor Choublanc's right-hand man, Aurelien Burnoldz-Mortier, has heatedly denounced "the teleguided intrusion by the cities of the East" of a slimy, evil Czechosoviet into the command post of our city. The young, brilliant Saint-Polycyrian also declared that he was convinced that Governor Choublanc had been "mentally coerced" and that his abdication occurred under "hypnosis". These facts were corroborated by Gogol d'Algol, telepathic advisor to Burnoldz-Mortier.

POSTE 1

"ORDER"

NO TO THE «FAKE» GOVERNOR

The Choublanquist government has refused outright to serve the "fake governor Alcide Nikopol" and resigned en masse yesterday evening. In an offical statement the members of the government have made known their intention of "rallying around one sole candidate so as to forge a new, inflexible spirit and to counter the ideological manipulations from outside aimed at the very basis of fascism". The sole candidate might well be, it is believed, Aurelien Burnoldz-Mortier, ex-governor Choublanc's confidant.

During the course of the afternoon the supreme selection committee will validate or reject the candidates. We should be reminded that this committee, presided over by Pope Theodule I, will announce the chosen candidates at 1 p.m. in the holy church of Notre-Dame of Paris... Besides the sitting governor and most likely Aurelien Burnoldz-Mortier, a limited number, 2 or 3 maximum, is expected to be selected in the light of the Choublanc affair and the current wave of extreme solidarity.

NOT EXACTLY A DAZZLING WELCOME FROM THE PRESS, IS IT? THERE'S ONLY ONE WAY I CAN SEE TO HOLD ONTO THIS POWER YOU WERE SO CLEVER IN SEIZING... HYPNOTIZE THE ENTIRE VOTING POPULATION...

ENOUGH SARCASM, NIKOPOL! I HAVE WAYS MAKING MORE MORTALS SEE REASON THAN EXIST IN THIS ENTIRE CITY... BUT I DON'T PLAN TO USE THEM EXCEPT AS A LAST RESORT...

FOR STARTERS I'LL BE CONTENT JUST TO ELIMINATE THE ONE OR MORE CANDIDATES PHYSICALLY... ONCE ALONE ON THE BALLOT WE'LL BE SURE TO BE RE-ELECTED...

TOMORROW WE'LL KNOW MORE ABOUT OUR OPPOSITION...

SAY, YOU'VE GOT SO MUCH POWER, DON'T YOU HAVE ANY-THING FOR SPLITTING MIGRAINES?

NEARBY, IN THE SUITE OF HIS HOLINESS POPE THEODULE I...

... HE SAYS THAT THE LEVITATOR IS READY AND THAT HE CAN GIVE YOU A DEMONSTRATION IF YOU WISH...

NO POINT... THE INSTRUCTIONS FOR USE WILL BE ENOUGH.

YOUR HOLINESS WILL BE ABLE TO RISE NEARLY 24 FEET OFF THE GROUND, HE WANTS YOU TO KNOW... AND WITH NO RISK... TO GET DOWN YOU ONLY HAVE TO PRESS A BUTTON...

THAT'S PERFECT... I THINK THIS IS AN OPPORTUNE MOMENT TO REINFORCE MY IMAGE AND MY CREDIBILITY IN THESE TROUBLED TIMES... THE CHURCH MUST BE EXALTED BY MY ACT... I WANT THIS "HANGING" OVER THE GROUND TO BE ATTRIBUTED TO A FORM OF DIVINE GRACE, A KIND OF MIRACLE... WITH THESE DEAR LITTLE CHERUBS SPINNING AROUND ME THE PICTURE WILL BE TOUCHING AND CONVINCING, I THINK

I THINK SO TOO, YOUR HOLINESS.

51

BUT UH... IN FACT AS FAR AS THESE LITTLE... CHERUBS ARE CONCERNED. I MUST DRAW YOUR HOLINESS'S ATTENTION TO THE WORRISOME RATE AT WHICH THEY ARE REPRODUCING AND...

NOW LET'S LET THESE HOLY CREATURES LEAD THEIR OWN LIVES...

NEXT DAY. A BEAUTIFUL DAY OF FOG AND RAIN...

WHAT YOU'VE MADE ME DO IS RIDICULOUS... IN MY DAY MEN DIDN'T

TSK TSK, IT'S UP TO US TO TAKE THE FIRST MOVE TOWARD THE VOTERS, NOT THEM TOWARD US...

WE'RE HERE, MR. GOVERNOR...

THE VOTERS DON'T GIVE A DAMN ABOUT OUR MOVES, JUST LIKE IN 1940.. AND THE POWERS THAT BE, THE REAL ONES, WILL USE OUR LITTLE DIVERSION TO MAKE THEIR DICTATORSHIP EVEN MORE BRUTAL AND PUT NEW MEN FORWARD WHO'LL PUSH US ASIDE, THEN WIPE US OUT...

YOU'RE FORGETTING TWO THINGS, NIKOPOL! FIRST, THAT I HAVE THE POWER TO HOLD ONTO POWER AND, SECONDLY, THAT I AM IMMORTAL...AND YOU AS WELL, AS LONG AS I LIVE IN YOUR BODY...

THAT'S IT, ETERNAL YOUTH! IMMORTALITY AFTER 30 YEARS OF HIBERNATION! DON'T BULLSHIT ME...

QUIET, NIKOPOL, QUIET...

54

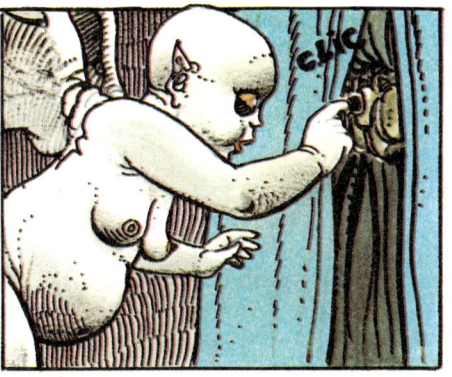

PLOTCH

...ARE YOU REALLY SURE THAT XB2 DIDN'T RECOGNIZE YOU... I MEAN ME?

CERTAIN!

...AND THAT'S WHAT MAKES ME BELIEVE THAT ANUBIS, BASTET AND THEIR FLUNKEYS HAVE ENTERED THE RACE... THIS ROBOT IS SHELTERING ONE OF THEM, I CAN SENSE IT...

IF I UNDERSTAND, THEN HE, TOO, HAS FALLEN INTO THE HANDS OF ONE OF YOU MADMEN... FUNNY HOW FATE HAD THE SAME JOYS IN STORE FOR US...

NO DOUBT THEY PREFERRED THE BODY OF A MACHINE RATHER THAN THAT OF A COMMON FLESH AND BLOOD MORTAL FOR ARCHAIC ETHICAL REASONS... BUT I DON'T CARE ABOUT THEIR METHODS... THEY WANT WAR!? THEY'LL GET IT...!!

"LIKE ANGELS WITH EYES OF WILD BEASTS, I'LL RETURN TO YOUR LOVE FEASTS SILENTLY HOLDING YOU TIGHT IN THE SHADOWS OF THE NIGHT..."

NOW I'LL SETTLE THINGS WITH BURNOLDZ-MORTIER AND XB2.... THINGS WILL BE CLEARER THEN...

"AND TO YOU, BRUNETTE, TIL I SWOON, I'LL GIVE KISSES COLD AS THE MOON"...

MY MIND IS MADE UP!

VLOUFF

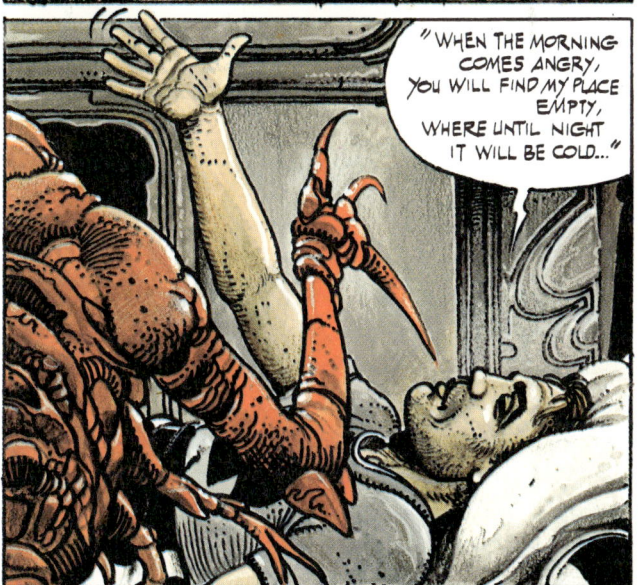

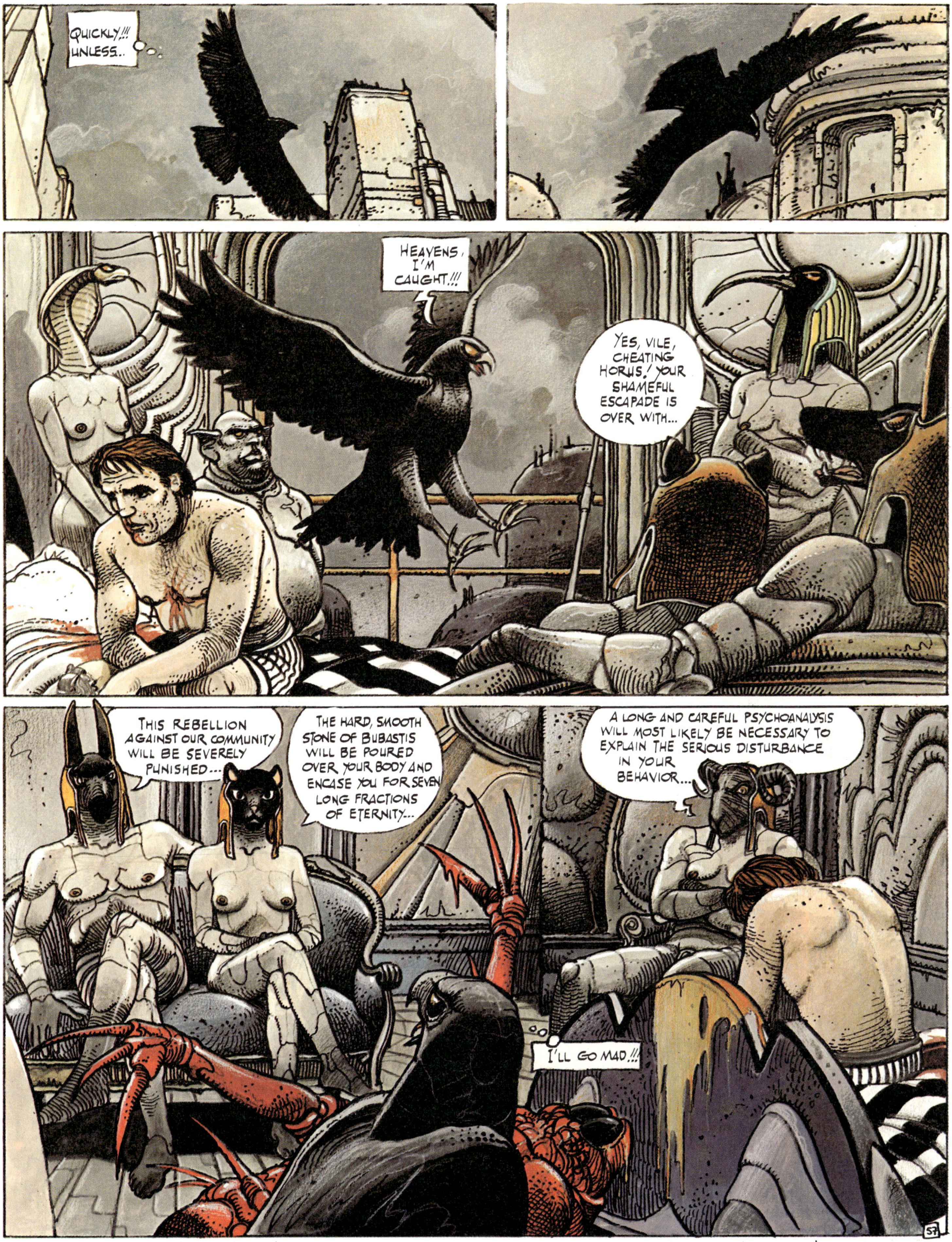

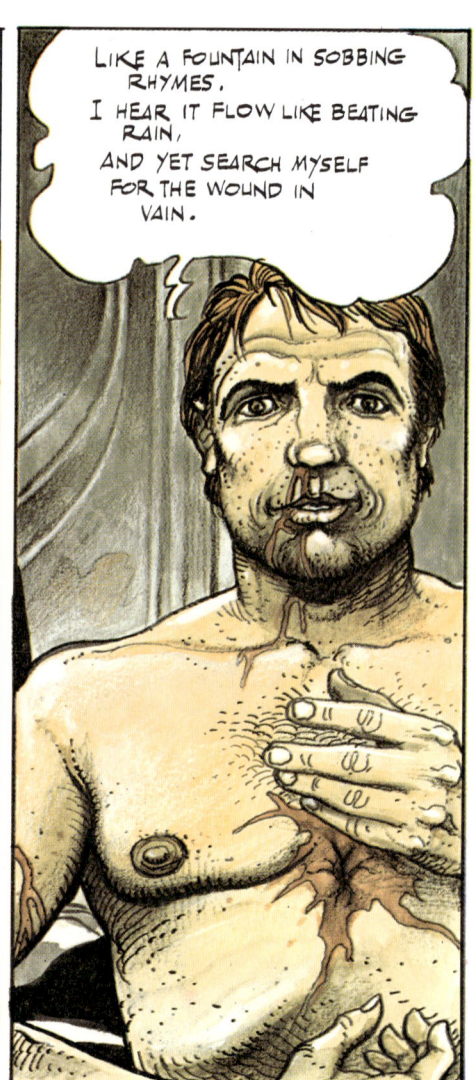

PARIS, MARCH 23, 2023. PRESS CLIPPINGS.

"SPIRIT OF REVOLUTION"

LEGALLY DISTRIBUTED — 160,000 COPIES PRINTED

FASCISM IS DEAD LONG LIVE NIKOPOL!

TODAY, MARCH 23, 2023, A HISTORIC DATE, A NEW ERA OF EQUALITY AND REVOLUTIONARY HOPE BEGINS FOR ALL PARISIANS UNITED AT LAST AS ONE. LET US THANK NIKOPOL, THE LIBERATOR OF PARIS, AND HOPE THAT THE STILL SMOLDERING ASHES OF THE CURSE OF FASCISM WILL BE SCATTERED IN THE WINDS OF HISTORY AND BE BLOTTED OUT FROM OUR TORTURED MEMORIES.

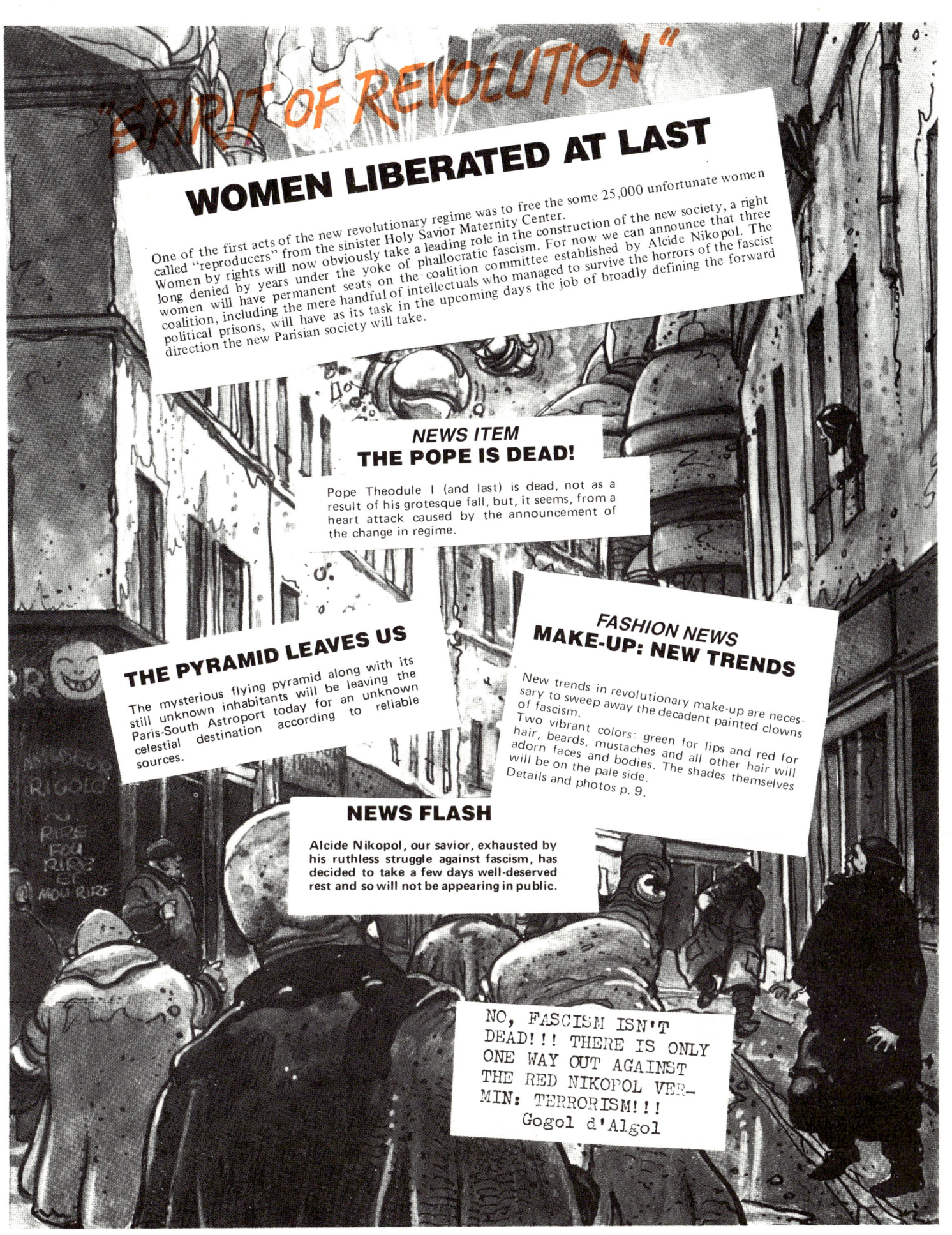

"SPIRIT OF REVOLUTION"

WOMEN LIBERATED AT LAST

One of the first acts of the new revolutionary regime was to free the some 25,000 unfortunate women called "reproducers" from the sinister Holy Savior Maternity Center. Women by rights will now obviously take a leading role in the construction of the new society, a right long denied by years under the yoke of phallocratic fascism. For now we can announce that three women will have permanent seats on the coalition committee established by Alcide Nikopol. The coalition, including the mere handful of intellectuals who managed to survive the horrors of the fascist political prisons, will have as its task in the upcoming days the job of broadly defining the forward direction the new Parisian society will take.

NEWS ITEM
THE POPE IS DEAD!

Pope Theodule I (and last) is dead, not as a result of his grotesque fall, but, it seems, from a heart attack caused by the announcement of the change in regime.

THE PYRAMID LEAVES US

The mysterious flying pyramid along with its still unknown inhabitants will be leaving the Paris-South Astroport today for an unknown celestial destination according to reliable sources.

FASHION NEWS
MAKE-UP: NEW TRENDS

New trends in revolutionary make-up are necessary to sweep away the decadent painted clowns of fascism.
Two vibrant colors: green for lips and red for hair, beards, mustaches and all other hair will adorn faces and bodies. The shades themselves will be on the pale side.
Details and photos p. 9.

NEWS FLASH

Alcide Nikopol, our savior, exhausted by his ruthless struggle against fascism, has decided to take a few days well-deserved rest and so will not be appearing in public.

NO, FASCISM ISN'T DEAD!!! THERE IS ONLY ONE WAY OUT AGAINST THE RED NIKOPOL VERMIN: TERRORISM!!!
Gogol d'Algol

THE SAME DAY, ABOVE THE CITY...

MARVIN GARDENS! I'LL BUY!!!

...AND IN THE CHAMBERS OF THE ELYSEE PALACE WHERE THE NEW REVOLUTIONARY POWER IS INSTALLED...

SO, WHAT ARE YOUR CONCLUSIONS, COMRADE DOCTOR?

IN MY EXPERIENCE THIS IS A CASE, WITHOUT PRECEDENT...

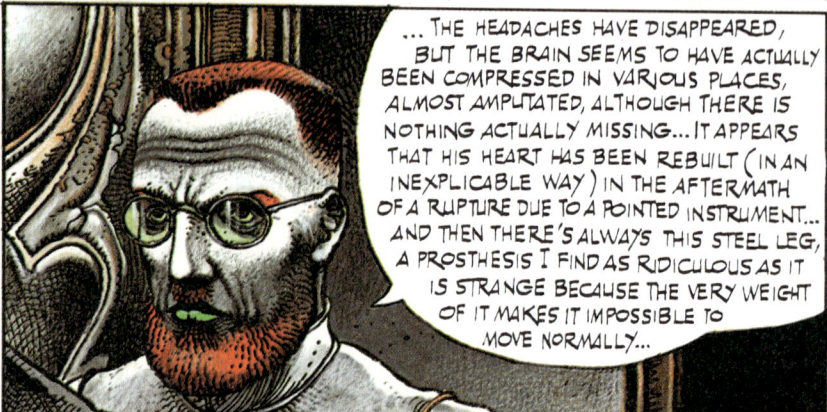

...THE HEADACHES HAVE DISAPPEARED, BUT THE BRAIN SEEMS TO HAVE ACTUALLY BEEN COMPRESSED IN VARIOUS PLACES, ALMOST AMPUTATED, ALTHOUGH THERE IS NOTHING ACTUALLY MISSING... IT APPEARS THAT HIS HEART HAS BEEN REBUILT (IN AN INEXPLICABLE WAY) IN THE AFTERMATH OF A RUPTURE DUE TO A POINTED INSTRUMENT... AND THEN THERE'S ALWAYS THIS STEEL LEG, A PROSTHESIS I FIND AS RIDICULOUS AS IT IS STRANGE BECAUSE THE VERY WEIGHT OF IT MAKES IT IMPOSSIBLE TO MOVE NORMALLY...

BUT THE MOST SERIOUS THING IS THE LOSS OF REASON BECAUSE I CAN'T SEE ANY WAY OF RECOVERY... THE POOR PATIENT SPENDS ALL DAY RECITING POETRY BY BAUDELAIRE, FLAT ON HIS BACK, STARING INTO SPACE, OR HE JUST BURSTS INTO LAUGHTER FOR NO REASON...

YEAH... HARD TO MAKE AN IDEOLOGICAL MODEL FOR THE PEOPLE...

HA HA HA HA HA HA...

THERE HE GOES AGAIN...

WHAT ARE WE GOING TO DO? ALL PARIS SEES HIM AS A HERO, A SAVIOR. AND THAT CAN'T BE DENIED, HE WAS THE ONE WHO STARTED IT ALL EVEN IF HIS BEHAVIOR BROUGHT TO BEAR ON HIS DEEPER POLITICAL ASPIRATIONS...

QUITE A MESS...

OUR POWER IS STILL TOO UNSTABLE TO...

LET ME THROUGH! GOD, I'M HIS SON!

WHAT'S GOING ON?

A CRAZY...

I AM NIKOPOL, ALCIDE NIKOPOL, ALCIDE NIKOPOL'S SON!

?!!

IN 1993, BEFORE I WAS BORN, HE WAS SENTENCED BY A MILITARY COURT TO 20 YEARS OF HIBERNATION IN SPACE... LIKE MANY REBELS IN HIS DAY HE SERVED AS A GUINEA PIG FOR A REVOLUTIONARY FLYING HIBERNATION VESSEL... SINCE THE WARS THAT FOLLOWED PRETTY MUCH BROUGHT AN END TO SCIENTIFIC PROGRAMS, HE WAS EITHER FORGOTTEN OR GIVEN UP ... ALL THIS TIME, OF COURSE, I WAS GROWING UP NORMALLY AND...

QUITE INTERESTING... ACCORDING TO SOME SOURCES IN THE MILITIA THE MYSTERIOUS VEHICLE SHOT DOWN THREE WEEKS AGO OVER THE 2ND SECTOR WAS IN FACT A TURN-OF-THE-CENTURY HIBERNATION MACHINE...

I THINK HE'S COME JUST IN TIME, COMRADES... WHAT DO YOU THINK?

HMMM... THE RESEMBLANCE IS STRIKING...

LISTEN, I KNOW IT MUST SOUND CRAZY THAT HE'S MY FATHER SINCE WE LOOK THE SAME AGE, BUT I CAN EXPLAIN EVERYTHING!

GO AHEAD THEN...

A FEW MINUTES LATER...

COMRADE NIKOPOL, HERE'S... UH, YOUR SON ALCIDE, WHO'S AGREED TO TAKE YOUR PLACE WHILE YOU RECOVER SO THAT UH... YOUR PRESENCE BEFORE THE NEW PARISIAN PEOPLE WILL CONTINUE IN A WAY...

DAD!?

... YOU PROBABLY DIDN'T EVEN KNOW I EXISTED... BUT I REALLY AM YOUR SON... YOURS AND CLEMENTINE MORGANIDON'S... I...

"OH YOU...

61

WEEKS PASSED. THE NEW COALITION, ORCHESTRATED BY AN UNUSUALLY DETERMINED ALCIDE NIKOPOL JR., WRESTLES FOR GOOD OR ILL WITH THE NEW EGALITARIAN SOCIETY...

ALONG WITH ECONOMIC AND ENERGY PROBLEMS HAVE COME THREATS OF INTERCITY WARS (ESPECIALLY WITH THE CITIES OF THE NORTH AND WEST).

ALONG WITH PROBLEMS OF CO-EXISTENCE WITH EXTRATERRESTRIAL RACES (THE NUMBER OF DIPHDA CHERUBS OCCUPYING NOTRE-DAME OF PARIS GROWS DAY BY DAY) HAVE COME TERRORIST ATTACKS BY REGROUPING FASCIST FACTIONS.

FINALLY, ALONG WITH THE PROBLEMS MET IN JOINING THE TWO SECTORS HAVE COME TERRIBLE RISKS OF EPIDEMIC AND MUTATIONS (DESPITE THE CLOSING OF THE ASTRO-PORT AND PRAISEWORTHY DESINFECTION CAMPAIGNS).

PARIS 2023, FRAGILE BUT FREE, PREPARES TO SAIL CLOSE TO SHORE ON VERY TROUBLED WATERS WITHOUT ITS LIBERATOR, THE UNFORTUNATE, THE LUCKLESS, THE PITIFUL ALCIDE NIKOPOL.

END

STORY · ILLUSTRATION · COLOR: BILAL